This book belongs to

______________________________

# Goldilocks and the Three Bears

RETOLD BY

Jennifer Greenway

ILLUSTRATED BY

Elizabeth Miles

ARIEL BOOKS

ANDREWS AND McMEEL
KANSAS CITY

 For information write Andrews and McMeel, a Universal Press Syndicate Company, 4900 Main Street, Kansas City, Missouri 64112.

Library of Congress Cataloging-in-Publication Data

Greenway, Jennifer.
Goldilocks and the three bears / retold by Jennifer Greenway ; illustrated by Elizabeth Miles.
p. cm.
Summary: Lost in the woods, a tired and hungry little girl finds the house of the three bears, where she helps herself to food and goes to sleep.
ISBN 0-8362-4900-3 (hd) : $6.95
[1. Folklore. 2. Bears—Folklore.] I. Miles, Elizabeth J., ill. II. Title.
III. Title: Goldilocks and the 3 bears.
PZ8.1.G858Go 1991
398.2—dc20
[E] 91-12560
CIP
AC

Design: Susan Hood and Mike Hortens
Art Direction: Armand Eisen, Mike Hortens, and Julie Phillips
Art Production: Lynn Wine
Production: Julie Miller and Lisa Shadid

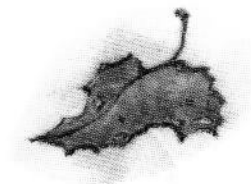

# Goldilocks and the Three Bears

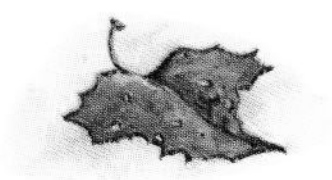

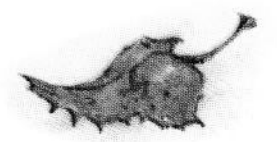

Once upon a time there were three bears who lived in a cottage in the woods. There was a great big Papa Bear, a medium-sized Mama Bear, and a little tiny Baby Bear.

One morning the three bears cooked themselves some porridge for breakfast. Then, as the porridge was much too hot to eat, they went for a walk in the woods while it cooled.

No sooner had they gone, than along came a little girl named Goldilocks.

Goldilocks had been playing in the woods and had gotten lost. When she saw the three bears' cottage, her eyes lit up.

"What a pretty little cottage," she said to herself. "I wonder who lives there?"

So Goldilocks went up to the cottage and knocked on the door. She waited quite a long time, but there was no answer.

Goldilocks walked around to the side of the cottage. She stood on her tiptoes, pressed her face to the window, and peered in. She could not see anyone. She stood still and listened carefully, but she could hear no one. So she hurried back to the front door, turned the knob, and walked in!

The first thing Goldilocks saw was a table set with three bowls of porridge. There was a great big bowl for Papa Bear, a medium-sized bowl for Mama Bear, and a little tiny bowl for Baby Bear.

Now Goldilocks was very fond of porridge, and her walk had made her hungry. So she took a taste of the porridge in the great big bowl.

But that porridge was much too hot!

"Ouch!" cried Goldilocks, dropping the spoon.

Next Goldilocks took a taste of the porridge in the medium-sized bowl.

But that porridge was much too cold!

"How nasty," said Goldilocks, making a horrible face. Then she took a taste of the porridge in the little tiny bowl.

That porridge was just right!

"Mmmm," said Goldilocks, with a smile. "This porridge is very tasty!" Then she took another spoonful and another and another. And before Goldilocks knew what she was doing, she had eaten Baby Bear's porridge all up!

Then Goldilocks saw three chairs set before the fireplace. There was a great big chair that belonged to Papa Bear, a medium-sized chair that belonged to Mama Bear, and a little tiny chair that belonged to Baby Bear.

Goldilocks climbed into Papa Bear's great big chair. "Ouch," she cried, jumping down at once. "That chair is much too hard!"

Next Goldilocks climbed into Mama Bear's medium-sized chair.

"Oh," she cried, as she sank down into the cushions. "This chair is much too soft!"

Then Goldilocks climbed into Baby Bear's little tiny chair.

"Ah," she said, and she smiled and leaned back. "This chair is just right!"

But just as Goldilocks was beginning to feel comfortable, down she tumbled with a crash!

"Oh dear," cried Goldilocks, for Baby Bear's little tiny chair was broken into a thousand pieces!

Next Goldilocks climbed the stairs to the three bears' bedroom. There she saw three beds all in a row. There was a great big bed for Papa Bear, a medium-sized bed for Mama Bear, and a little tiny bed for Baby Bear.

First, Goldilocks climbed into Papa Bear's great big bed and pulled down the covers.

But she jumped down right away.

"Oh no," Goldilocks said. "That bed is much too hard!"

Then she climbed into Mama Bear's medium-sized bed. "Oh dear," said Goldilocks, wrinkling her nose. "This bed is much too soft!"

Then Goldilocks went to Baby Bear's little tiny bed, pulled down the covers, and climbed in.

That bed was just right!

Goldilocks closed her eyes, and soon she was fast asleep.

Then the three bears returned from their walk. They were very hungry and were looking forward to a breakfast of delicious porridge.

As soon as they came inside, the three bears washed their hands and sat down at the table.

Papa Bear stared down at his great big bowl. Then he said in his great big voice, "Someone has been eating my porridge!"

Mama Bear looked down at her bowl. "Oh dear," she said in her medium-sized voice, "someone has been eating *my* porridge!"

Then Baby Bear looked down at his little tiny bowl. "Someone has been eating *my* porridge," he cried in his little tiny voice, "and they've eaten it all up!"

Then the three bears walked to their three chairs that were set before the fireplace.

Just as Papa Bear was about to sit down in his great big chair, he growled in his great big voice, "Someone has been sitting in my chair!"

And just as Mama Bear was about to sit down in her medium-sized chair, she cried out in her medium-sized voice, "Someone has been sitting in *my* chair!"

Baby Bear looked down at his little tiny chair. "Someone has been sitting in *my* chair," he cried in his little tiny voice, "and they've broken it into a thousand pieces!"

Next the three bears went upstairs to the bedroom.

Papa Bear looked at his great big bed and saw that the covers had been pulled down. Then he frowned and growled in his great big voice, "Someone has been sleeping in my bed!"

Then Mama Bear looked at her medium-sized bed and saw that the pillows had been scattered about.

"And someone has been sleeping in *my* bed," Mama Bear cried in her medium-sized voice.

Baby Bear looked at his little tiny bed. "And someone has been sleeping in *my* bed!" he cried in his little tiny voice, "AND HERE SHE IS!"

When Goldilocks heard Baby Bear's little tiny voice, she awoke with a start. She looked up and saw the three bears standing around her.

Goldilocks was so frightened that she leaped out of bed, raced down the stairs, and dashed out the door of the three bears' cottage. And she didn't stop running until she was all the way home.

Then the three bears fixed themselves another breakfast of hot porridge. And they never saw Goldilocks again!